KU-862-885

This book belongs to:

BERWYN

A catalogue record for this book is available from the British Library

Published by Ladybird Books Ltd
80 Strand London WC2R 0RL
A Penguin Company

6 8 10 9 7

© Ladybird Books Ltd MMV

Endpaper map illustrations by Fred van Deelen

LADYBIRD and the device of a Ladybird are trademarks of Ladybird Books Ltd

All rights reserved. No part of this publication may be reproduced,
stored in a retrieval system, or transmitted in any form or by any means,
electronic, mechanical, photocopying, recording or otherwise,
without the prior consent of the copyright owner.

ISBN-13: 978-1-84422-300-8
ISBN-10: 1-84422-300-0

Printed in Italy

LADYBIRD TALES

The Three Billy Goats Gruff

Retold by Vera Southgate M.A., B.Com

with illustrations by David Kearney

Once upon a time there were three billy goats called Gruff.

One fine day, the three billy goats Gruff set off up the hillside. They were going to look for some sweet grass to eat.

On the way up the hillside, the three billy goats Gruff came to a river.

On the other side of the river was a beautiful meadow. In the meadow was the finest grass they had ever seen.

There was a wooden bridge over the river, but under the bridge there lived an ugly troll. People were afraid to cross the bridge because of the troll.

Every time he heard footsteps on the bridge, he popped out and gobbled up the person who was trying to cross.

The three billy goats Gruff were very frightened at the thought of the troll. Yet they longed to eat the sweet grass in the meadow on the other side of the river.

After a while, the youngest billy goat Gruff said that he would be the first to try and cross the bridge.

Trip, trap, trip, trap went the hooves of the youngest billy goat Gruff on the wooden bridge.

Out popped the troll's ugly head. He was so ugly that the youngest billy goat Gruff nearly fell down with fright.

"Who's that trip-trapping over my bridge?" roared the troll.

The youngest billy goat Gruff spoke in a tiny voice. "It's only me, the littlest billy goat Gruff," he said. "I'm going to the meadow to eat the sweet grass."

"Then I'm coming to gobble you up," roared the troll.

"Oh no! Please don't gobble me up," said the youngest billy goat Gruff in a tiny voice. "I'm far too little and not at all tasty. Wait until the second billy goat Gruff comes along. He's much more tasty than I am."

"Very well," said the troll.
"Be off with you! I'll wait until
the second billy goat Gruff
comes along."

So the youngest billy goat Gruff
crossed the bridge and skipped
off into the meadow to eat the
sweet grass.

Then the second billy goat Gruff
said that he would try to cross
the bridge.

Trip, *trap*, *trip*, *trap* went the hooves of the second billy goat Gruff on the wooden bridge.

Out popped the troll's ugly head. He was so ugly that the second billy goat Gruff nearly fell down with fright.

"Who's that trip-trapping over my bridge?" roared the troll.

The second billy goat Gruff spoke in a rather soft voice. "It's only me, the second billy goat Gruff," he said. "I'm going to the meadow to eat the sweet grass."

"Then I'm coming to gobble you up," roared the troll.

"Oh no! Please don't gobble me up," said the second billy goat Gruff, in his rather soft voice. "I'm not very big and I'm not very tasty. Wait until the third billy goat Gruff comes along. He's very big and very tasty."

"Very well," said the troll. "Be off with you! I'll wait until the third billy goat Gruff comes along."

So the second billy goat Gruff crossed the bridge and skipped off into the meadow to eat the sweet grass.

Then, at last, the eldest billy goat Gruff came up to try to cross the bridge.

He was a very big billy goat. His beard was long and his horns were almost fully grown.

TRIP, TRAP,
TRIP, TRAP,
BANG, BANG,
BANG, BANG,

went the hooves of the eldest billy
goat Gruff on the wooden bridge.

Out popped the troll's ugly head. He was so ugly that the eldest billy goat Gruff nearly fell down with fright.

But he did not show it. He only stamped his hooves harder:

TRIP, TRAP,
TRIP, TRAP,
BANG, BANG,
BANG, BANG.

"Who's that trip-trapping over my bridge?" roared the troll.

The eldest billy goat Gruff's voice was even louder and gruffer than the troll's voice. "It's me, the biggest billy goat Gruff," he bellowed.

"Then I'm coming to gobble you up," roared the troll.

"Oh no, you are not!" bellowed the eldest billy goat Gruff. "I am coming to gobble *you* up!"

And he stamped his feet even louder:

TRIP, TRAP,
TRIP, TRAP,
BANG, BANG,
BANG, BANG

After that, the eldest billy goat Gruff butted the troll with his big horns.

The ugly troll fell off the bridge head first into the deep water. There was a mighty splash and the troll disappeared, never to be seen again.

So that was the end of the ugly troll.

From that time on, people went over the bridge without fear.

Never again did the troll pop his head out from under the bridge to roar, "Who's that trip-trapping over my bridge?"

The three billy goats Gruff lived happily ever after in the meadow on the hillside. They ate the sweet grass and they were never hungry again.